Titles in Series S892

Little Tommy Tucker and other nursery rhymes
Little Jack Horner and other nursery rhymes
Little Bo Peep and other nursery rhymes
Little Miss Muffet and other nursery rhymes

British Library Cataloguing in Publication Data
Little Miss Muffet and other nursery rhymes.
  I. Bracken, Carolyn
  398'.8
  ISBN 0-7214-9593-1

First edition
Published by Ladybird Books Ltd Loughborough Leicestershire UK
Ladybird Books Inc Auburn Maine 04210 USA
Printed in England

Little Miss Muffet
and other nursery rhymes

Illustrated by Carolyn Bracken

Ladybird Books

Old Mother Hubbard went to the cupboard,
To fetch her poor dog a bone;
But when she got there the cupboard was bare
And so the poor dog had none.

Little Miss Muffet sat on a tuffet,
Eating her curds and whey;
There came a big spider, who sat down beside her
And frightened Miss Muffet away.

Peter, Peter, pumpkin eater,
Had a wife and couldn't keep her;
He put her in a pumpkin shell,
And there he kept her very well.

Peter, Peter, pumpkin eater,
Had another, and didn't love her;
Peter learned to read and spell,
And then he loved her very well.

Baa, baa, black sheep, have you any wool?
Yes, sir, yes, sir, three bags full;
One for the master and one for the dame,
And one for the little boy
        who lives down the lane.

Curly Locks, Curly Locks, will you be mine?
You shall not wash dishes, nor yet feed the swine;
But sit on a cushion and sew a fine seam,
And feed upon strawberries, sugar and cream.

Bobby Shaftoe's gone to sea,
Silver buckles on his knee;
He'll come back and marry me,
Bonny Bobby Shaftoe!

Bobby Shaftoe's bright and fair,
Combing down his yellow hair;
He's my love forevermore,
Bonny Bobby Shaftoe!

Barber, barber, shave a pig,
How many hairs will make a wig?
Four and twenty, that's enough;
Give the barber a pinch of snuff.

Dickery, dickery, dare,
The pig flew up in the air;
The man in brown
Soon brought him down,
Dickery, dickery, dare.

Little Betty Blue lost her holiday shoe;
What can little Betty do?
Give her another to match the other,
And then she may walk out in two.

Simple Simon met a pieman
Going to the fair;
Said Simple Simon to the pieman,
"Let me taste your ware."

Said the pieman to Simple Simon,
"Show me first your penny."
Said Simple Simon to the pieman,
"Indeed, I have not any."

When I was a little boy,
I washed my mother's dishes;
Now I am a great big boy,
I roll in golden riches.

When I was a little boy,
I washed my mother's floor;
Now I am a man of wealth,
And drive a coach and four.

Jack Sprat could eat no fat,
His wife could eat no lean,
And so between them both, you see,
They licked the platter clean.

The lion and the unicorn
Were fighting for the crown;
The lion beat the unicorn
All around the town.

Some gave them white bread,
And some gave them brown;
Some gave them plum cake,
And drummed them out of town.

Baby and I were baked in a pie,
The gravy was wonderful hot.
We had nothing to pay to the baker that day
And so we crept out of the pot.

Nose, nose, jolly red nose,
What gave you that jolly red nose?
Nutmeg and ginger, cinnamon and cloves,
That's what gave me this jolly red nose.

Cock-a-doodle-doo!
My dame has lost her shoe,
My master's lost his fiddling stick
And doesn't know what to do.

Cock-a-doodle-doo!
What is my dame to do?
Till master finds his fiddling stick
She'll dance without her shoe.

Cock-a-doodle-doo!
My dame has found her shoe,
And master's found his fiddling stick,
Sing doodle-doodle-doo.

Cock-a-doodle-doo!
My dame will dance with you,
While master fiddles his fiddling stick
For dame and doodle-doo.

Yankee Doodle went to town,
Riding on a pony;
He stuck a feather in his cap
And called it macaroni.

I had a little pony,
His name was Dapple Gray;
I lent him to a lady
To ride a mile away.
She whipped him, she slashed him,
She rode him through the mire;
I would not lend my pony now,
For all the lady's hire.

There was a crooked man,
And he walked a crooked mile,
He found a crooked sixpence
Against a crooked stile;
He bought a crooked cat,
Which caught a crooked mouse,
And they all lived together
In a little crooked house.

Star light, star bright,
First star I see tonight,
I wish I may, I wish I might,
Have the wish I wish tonight.

How many miles to Babylon?
Three score miles and ten.
Can I get there by candlelight?
Yes, and back again.
If your heels are nimble and light,
You may get there by candlelight.

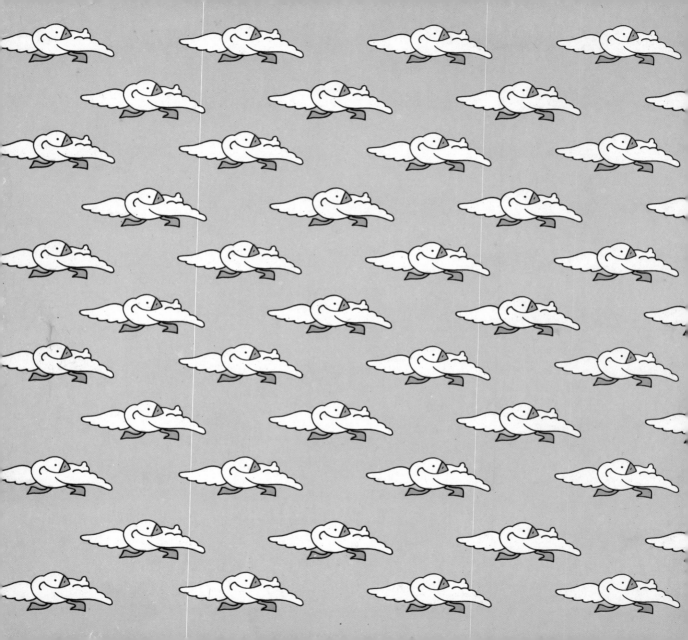